Falling in Love

Sheila H   andy Perez and
Adam A   or,
Illustrated   h Webb

First published in Great Britain 1999 by St George's Hospital
Medical School and Gaskell.

ISBN 1-901242-32-3

British Library Cataloguing-in-Publication Data.
A catalogue record for this book is available from the
British Library.

Distributed in North America
by American Psychiatric Press, Inc.
ISBN 0-88048-965-0

Printed and bound in Great Britain by Bell & Bain Limited,
Thornliebank, Glasgow G46 7UQ.

Further information about the Books Beyond Words series can
be obtained from:

Royal College of Psychiatrists
17 Belgrave Square
London SW1X 8PG

Tel: 0171 235 2351
Fax: 0171 245 1231

Acknowledgements

We would like to thank our editorial advisers, Nigel Hollins and Lloyd Page; the Women's Group and staff at Blakes & Link Employment Agency (Hammersmith & Fulham Social Services); and the Men's Group and staff at Lifecare NHS Trust.

We are also grateful to Valerie Sinason and Alice Thacker who gave their time most generously to help us.

Our special thanks to art assistant, Linda Nash.

The story

1. Barbara and Janet were chatting.

2. Mike and Harry said "Hello".

3. Harry knew Barbara. Janet said "Hello". She did not know Mike.

4. Harry and Barbara were sitting close together. Janet and Mike were getting to know each other.

5. They all thought about going to the cinema.

6. They were eating popcorn in the cinema.

7. "Sh-sh!" "Don't spoil the film".

8. The usher told them to leave. They came out of the cinema. They were upset.

9. The girls were falling in love.

10. Janet wanted to ring Mike. She felt shy. Mike wanted to phone Janet. Harry said "Go on".

11. Mike and Janet talked on the phone.

12. Mike came to Janet's house.

13. Janet and Mike wanted to be alone. Barbara wanted to watch TV.

14. Mike said "Goodbye". Janet wanted him to stay.

15. Janet went to Mike's house. He opened the door.

16. Janet met Mike's Dad.

17. Dad went out – then they were alone.

18. Mike and Janet were kissing.

19. Mike said "Come to bed with me".

20. Janet turned away. She said "No". She didn't want to go to bed.

21. It was hard to talk. Both felt shy and a bit hurt.

22. Then they were talking.

23. They listened to music together.

24. Janet introduced Mike to her Mum and Dad.

25. Mike and Janet enjoyed lots of things together. They walked in the park and went to the seaside. At Christmas they gave each other presents.

26. They went window shopping. Mike watched football. Janet looked at wedding dresses.

27. They were talking about getting married.

28. Janet's parents were worried. What would happen in the future? "Where will you live?" "What about money?" "And what if you have a baby?"

29. Janet and Barbara talked about things. Janet talked about getting engaged and getting married. They talked about sex, birth control and babies. They wondered where Janet and Mike would live.

30. Mike and Harry talked about the same things.

31. Mike and Janet loved each other. They decided to get married.

32. They chose an engagement ring.

33. Mike put the ring on Janet's finger.

34. They told Janet's parents.

35. They told Harry and Barbara.

36. Mike and Janet were happy together.

37. Mike and Janet planned their future.

38. Everyone said "Congratulations!"

Love

Loving is part of being human, and so is touching and being touched. Sex is a natural part of this, and the part we often find most difficult for ourselves, let alone trying to advise anyone else.

People may need practical support as well as good advice about making friends and enjoying close and intimate relationships. This can create unique complications for parents and others who also wish to provide care and protection, but may not like their grown-up children's choices. If their child has a learning disability this can make it harder to allow a 'dignity of risk'. In the wish to protect, parents may be unaware they are stifling normal growth.

Some parents may feel more comfortable than others when discussing personal matters with their son or daughter. Others may find it helpful to talk to someone else who knows him or her well, explaining any concerns they have. Most important of all, their son or daughter should be encouraged to speak about these personal things, which they may think are taboo.

Hurt

Relationships can be painful and most of us can remember a time when we felt sad, lonely, angry, scared or lost because a loving relationship had come to an end. This sort of pain is part of being alive and when we try to protect someone, it takes away precious freedoms as well.

All young adults require privacy to develop emotionally and sexually. Where privacy is not provided, important areas of growth are spoilt or distorted. People with learning disabilities should have the chance to make ordinary mistakes, just as we all do. Their reward will be the opportunity to experience joy, excitement and fun as well.

Healthy and appropriate sexual expression should not be restricted, because people who are kept in ignorance are more likely to show disturbed behaviour or to be abused.

Culture

This book cannot hope to reflect the wide diversity of religious, ethnic and moral views and choices in our society.

- Parents and carers will still need to think the issues through for themselves.

- It will help to have a confident, open and explicit approach to the subject.

Legality, permission and consent

People often mix up these three concepts, and professionals in particular worry that they may be allowing something which is against the law. It is probably best to think about one's duty of care. Health and safety are very important. Above all, despite all practical concerns and social taboos, it is important to remember what a gift human loving (including sexual love) is for everyone's health and happiness.

The most important concept is consent. Consent can sometimes be very complicated – for instance, someone consenting to medical treatment needs to know about side-effects, reasons for treatment and so on. But establishing consent to be in a relationship and to take part in intimate activity is usually much simpler. People generally demonstrate their consent by their actions.

If you can answer 'yes' to all the questions below, then you should probably be supporting the relationship:

- Do both people in the relationship have learning disabilities?

- Are both people in the relationship able to make decisions and act independently in another area of daily living? Such as:
  - *being able to show pleasure in any one activity*
  - *having clear preferences in diet or in which TV programmes they watch*

- *enjoying other social activities such as games and entertainment in company*
- *making decisions about what to wear*
- *holding a conversation, or using gestures or other body language to communicate.*

- Has the relationship grown over time?

- Are both people more or less equally active in maintaining contact with each other?

- Do you think there is a reasonable balance of power between the partners?

- Do both people seem to enjoy the relationship?

- Do both people appear happy in their relationship?

- Have safe sex and contraceptive precautions been taken?

If you answered 'no' to any of these questions, what can you do to reduce any possible harmful effects in the relationship? For example, does one of the partners need to learn how to express their wishes more clearly?

If you do not feel a relationship is safe or healthy, what guidance do the partners need? It is probably best to engage both people in a dialogue, and try to help them understand your concerns.

As with any other activity, staff and carers should:

- Assess and minimise any risks, and maintain their duty of care.

- Help adults with learning disabilities to achieve a good quality of life.

- Encourage them to develop their competence to choose.

- Show respect for their individuality and dignity.

Who to contact for help and advice

Community Teams for People with Learning Disabilities (CTPLDs) These are specialist multi-disciplinary health teams that support adults with learning disabilities and their families by assessment of their needs and a range of interventions, including relationship counselling and advice on contraception.

Social Service Departments Social Service departments manage and purchase social care, for example, housing and day services for people with learning disabilities.

Ann Craft Trust (formerly NAPSAC) **Tel: 0115 951 5400**
Centre for Social Work
University of Nottingham
Nottingham
NG7 2RD

Provides advice and training for the caring professions on sexuality and learning disabilities and on sexual abuse.

British Association of Counselling **Tel: 01788 578328**
1 Regents Place
Rugby
Coventry
CV21 2PJ

The British Association of Counselling maintains the register of all trained counsellors in the UK.

Consent **Tel: 01923 670796**
Woodside Road
Abbots Langley
Hertfordshire
WD5 0HT

Provides consultancy, sexuality education and training.

Family Planning Association   **Tel: 0171 837 4044**
2/12 Pentonville Road
London
N1 9FP

The telephone helpline provides family planning advice.

Respond   **Tel: 0171 383 0700**
3rd Floor
24-32 Stephenson Way
London
NW1 2HD

Provides advice, consultation and treatment in sexuality issues
for learning disabled service users.

VOICE UK   **Tel: 01332 519872**
PO Box 238
Derby
DE1 9JN

Provides support and information for people with learning
disabilities who have been abused and hurt and for their
families and carers.

Books and videos

How to form new relationships is the subject of two other titles in the Books Beyond Words series: *Hug Me, Touch Me* (1994) and *Making Friends* (1995) By Sheila Hollins and Terry Roth. Available at £10 each (including p&p) from the Royal College of Psychiatrists, 17 Belgrave Square, London SW1X 8PG. Tel: 0171 235 2351 extension 146.

Everything You Ever Wanted to Know About Safer Sex But Nobody Ever Bothered to Tell You (1994) Produced by People First. Format: audio cassette (30 minutes); booklet (20 pages). Price: £11.00 plus p&p. From: People First, Instrument House, 207–215 Kings Cross Road, London WC1X 9DB. Tel: 0171 713 6400.

My Choice, My Own Choice (1992) A safer sex video for people with learning difficulties. Produced by the South East London Health Promotion Service and enacted by actors with learning difficulties. Video (25 minutes). Two teaching packs include line drawings, exercises and role plays. £55 plus VAT. From: Pavilion Publishing, 8 St George's Place, Brighton, East Sussex BN1 4GB. Tel: 01273 623222.

A wide range of other titles, videos etc. on sexuality and relationships, are reviewed in *Health Related Resources for People with Learning Disabilities* (1995). Available at £5.99 from the Health Education Authority, PO Box 269, Abingdon, Oxfordshire OX14 4YN. Tel: 01235 465565.